BEDTIME STORIES

for Stressed-Out Adults

Meditation Short Stories to Self-Healing, Reduce and Relieve Stress, and Overcame Anxiety

Kaden Wolf

author is not engaging in the rendering of legal, financial, medical or professional advice. The content within this book has been derived from various sources. Please consult a licensed professional before attempting any techniques outlined in this book.

By reading this document, the reader agrees that under no circumstances is the author responsible for any losses, direct or indirect, which are incurred as a result of the use of information contained within this document, including, but not limited to, errors, omissions, or inaccuracies.

Table of Contents

Introduction

Congratulations on purchasing *Bedtime Stories for Adults* and thank you for doing so.

This book has carefully selected stories that will help you to relax at the end of a long day right before you go to sleep.

There are quite a number of books which have been written about this topic that is readily available on the market and thank you for choosing this particular one. In the making of this book, every effort was made to ensure that it is full of as much useful information as possible, and please enjoy it!

Forsaken Among the Forsaken

Hurry up Foden, else you'll be late for school Mr. Adams admonished as he stepped into his black Mercedes Benz ready to convey his only son Foden to school. Although he had made everything possible to ensure Foden improved academically, his son simply wasn't cut out for academic work. He was either too lazy to pursue his academic dreams or simply did not have the zest to do so. In a jiffy, Foden dashed out of the house dragging his schoolbag behind him. If there was a world competition for the best-dressed student, Foden would be up there among the top three if not the best dressed. His school uniform always sparkled, with seemingly unreplaceable ghetto lines.

In school, Foden wasn't the brightest. His teachers would often downplay his little efforts. His classmates didn't help matters also, they would often mock and make jest of him whenever he failed a question in class. Having been registered for extramural classes in his school, it is safe to conclude his parents wanted the best for him. Despite the frantic efforts put in by his parents to help him academically, it never translated into academic success for him.

Foden's mum was a full-time housewife. She stayed behind at home when her husband goes to work every day. Unlike her son, she was quite hardworking and committed to making the home a happy one. For over 12 years of her marriage, she literally sat at home every day performing household chores. It was one job she loved doing, but she was getting tired of repeating the same routine every other day. She wanted a new experience, a new dimension, and a feel of what the professional world of business looks like. Although her husband initially debunked the idea, she persisted and she eventually got her way.

Foden was trying so hard to make an impression in class on a bright Tuesday morning. His teacher Mrs. West had put forward a question to the class. Mrs. West was their English teacher; though playful she could be very strict when necessary. Yes, you Foden she said as she pointed at Foden who had been raising his hands as an indication for his willingness to attempt the question. We stood up enthusiastically and gave the answer to the question. Whether he was right or not, he couldn't tell for a split second as the class was mute as if silence passed the classroom. Foden was left red-faced as his classmates rent the air with laughter. Obviously, it wasn't the laughter of approval or satisfaction. It was that of sheer mockery, downgrading, and morale-sapping. To Foden's consternation, his teacher was also visibly smiling. Among all his teachers, his English teacher would never openly laugh at him. At this point Foden felt completely alone, the laughter from his classmates was overshadowed by a grave feeling of solitude. Foden had never felt this dejected, he slumped back to his seat ashamed.

Mrs. West managed to curtail the laughter of the class and restored decorum, but the damage was already done. For the rest of the class, Foden was quiet. He didn't speak to anyone and no one bothered speaking to him. They rather cracked funny jokes about him and made a further jest of him. The school bell rang at about 3:00 p.m., which served as a mark of the closure of school activities for that day. With no friend to share his feelings with or console him at least, he stood alone in the terrace patiently waiting for his father's car to arrive. Before long, his father's car pulled over like a messiah as some group of students was walking towards his direction. He could only assume what they had in mind, perhaps to mock him again for his failures. At least this was not to be as he hurriedly raced to his father's car.

The time on the huge clock which hung on the wall opposite the entrance door of the sitting room was 6:05 p.m. Mrs. Adams would have been back by now, how come she isn't home yet? Mr. Adams wondered. Perhaps she has been stuck with work yet again. This was becoming quite unbearable for him. He never bought the idea of letting his wife work outside the home though she was a chartered accountant by profession. A few weeks ago, the dinner would have been ready by this time, but here he was, famished with absolutely little or no idea on how to conjure up the magic his wife usually did which led to those sumptuous meals.

Just as Foden and his father were struggling to piece together some food ingredients to make dinner, their savior arrived. It was Mrs. Adams looking all stressed out from her work. She couldn't wait to freshen up and rescue his husband and son from the kitchen. Left for her though, she simply would have taken a cold shower and toss herself on the bed.

As usual, it took Mrs. Adams wasted very little time in preparing the meal, and goodness me, was it delicious?

Of course, it was her trademark. On this occasion, however, Mr. Adams just wasn't happy not because of the food, but because of the recent lateness of his wife in closing from work. He was further bothered about his son's reluctance to hold a reasonable conversation since he came back from school. Mr. Adams didn't wait behind, as usual, to watch his favorite TV shows before going to bed. Instead, he went off to bed immediately after eating. This was something he rarely does and it was a clear indication that he wasn't happy.

Over the next few weeks, Mrs. Adams turned a new leaf, she no longer closed late from work. She prepared breakfast and dinner as at when due as usual. The Adams family was back to the happy home they used to be earlier saved for the woman doing a professional job and Foden being more taciturn. In the cool of a Friday evening, Mr. Adam decided to pay his wife a surprise visit at her office. Anyway, it was already a few minutes past her closing hours and it was weekend. He wanted to give her a surprise treat. Zoom, he went off as he throttled furiously on the less busy road that linked his house to his wife's working place.

On entering into the complex, he didn't find it difficult to locate his wife's office. His wife was very good at description and has somehow managed to vividly describe where she worked. I believe I description of the building would be matched only by the architect himself who drew the plan. Mr. Foden was left disappointed as he knocked severally on his wife's office door with no response. Perhaps she had gone home earlier than usual. He decided to seize this rare opportunity to have a better look at the magnificent building as the staff was trooping out in twos and threes. He came across an office with its door slightly ajar, he was overtaken by over curiosity. All the office he had passed through were either locked or fully opened, why was this particular door slightly open? He decided to peep and satisfy his curiosity.

For the next few seconds, Mr. Adams simply stood there transfixed. He could not believe what his eyes have seen neither could his brain properly discern what was happening. Perhaps this was a symptom of blindness or he fell into a trance. He took out his white handkerchief which had been tucked away neatly in his back pocket and wiped his face to be doubly sure he wasn't going blind. After staring for a few more minutes he furiously dashed out of the complex as if chased by fierce masquerades. He canceled every other plan he had for the night including the treat. There were more things more important than the others, he had to attend urgently to what had earlier left him bedazzled.

The tires of his car screeched as he furiously made a U-turn on impulse. He headed straight to one of his friend's apartment. He couldn't comprehensively share with his friends what his eyes had seen. He was still in shock and can't still get to believe that was what goes on in Cashmore Ltd where his wife worked. The essence of driving about 1km in the opposite direction of his house was utterly defeated as Desmond failed to make out exactly what his friend was saying. However, he resolved to calm him and down probably ask for a better explanation when he gets calmer and more collected.

For the very first time since the day Foden was admitted to a hospital in an emergency, Mr. Adams failed to get back home. Both Foden and his mum were worried sick and attempts made to contact Mr. Adams ended in utter futility. Mrs. Adams's mind was slightly relaxed when he finally contacted Desmond and he told her Mr. Adams was just leaving his apartment. Why his husband would drive down to see Desmond on a Friday night was beyond her imagination. Still, she kept her fingers crossed and expected her husband to come back home all through the night, but that was not to be.

Foden was further plunged into the depths of loneliness and solitude in class. At some point, he contemplated suicide without his parent's knowledge, but he didn't know exactly how to go about it as he was still young. His teachers in school never helped matters at all. The last stroke which broke the camel's back came the day his principal mistakenly left him in detention from morning until school closing hours for performing poorly in class. He learned absolutely nothing, completely abandoned in the principal's office at the mercy of the big bullies in school.

As they say, every disappointment is a blessing. This was the case of Foden that particular day. Instead of the big bullies who regularly piled on the misery on him to continue from where they left off, they rather sympathized with him and told him words of comfort. Every one of them there had committed one grave offense or the other which violated the school's rules and regulations, but Foden to the best of their knowledge did nothing but perform poorly in his academics. Soon Foden found solace in their company. Though he knew they were all members of a bad gang, he had no choice than to mingle with them. He had been forsaken for far too long by those who were supposed to have his back.

Court proceeding started that beautiful Monday morning with the judge ruling the first case in favor of a famous artist who had been accused of rape and second-degree murder. Next up was the case filed by Mr. Foden, he had acted on the advice of his friend Desmond. Till this point, Foden was lost in the dark, not knowing why exactly his father had filed a court case. Anyway, he calmed his nerves as he was about to find out in a jiffy. Mrs. Adams do you plead guilty or not guilty, the judge repeated for the third time, jolting Mrs. Adams back to reality. She had been lost in thoughts and tears slowly rolled down her eyes.

How she wished she could change the hands of time to when her husband refused to grant her permission to practice her profession. She would have grabbed the disapproval with both hands. She wept bitterly at the thoughts of her actions, but here she was facing reality. She had no choice but to respond soberly to the judge. Mrs. Adams pleaded not guilty to the divorce case filed by her husband on the grounds of infidelity. Mrs. Adams knew fully well this was a last-ditch effort to salvage her home.

The prosecutor's attorney stepped forward and tendered a cassette disk that contained a video of the illicit act Mrs.

Adams had with her boss in the office. There wouldn't be any better glaring evidence that this. The judge ruled the divorce case in favor of Mr. Adams and dissolved the marriage which otherwise was a happy one until a few weeks ago. Foden was given a choice to choose any of the parents he will live with. For a young boy like Foden to make such a decision was a very difficult call. Again, he had to face reality, he had to make a choice right there and then. Though he loved his mum dearly, her actions were really disappointed thus he decided to live with his father. He really wished he didn't make the wrong call.

Foden had to cope with the constant mockery at school and his stepmother who always treated him badly regardless of what he did. Things were becoming so unbearable for Foden. He would often trek long distances to and fro school while his father attended to the needs of his stepbrother. Little did he know this was just the beginning of his ordeal. This went from bad to worse real quick and he could hardly believe his eyes the day his father threw him out of the house. It was a chilled winter evening; with such unconducive weather, he was tossed out of his home.

It was already getting late, he had absolutely no precise place to head to neither did he know anyone who could help him. He had been forsaken by his very own family. His life prior to this moment had been basically a boring triangle of school to home to church and repeat. Just as he languidly crossed the road to the other side, a thought flashed through his mind. One of the bullies had invited him to a party downtown. Perhaps he should go there and look for them. He quickly made up and his mind and headed for the party venue.

Luckily for him, he got a free lift. On getting to the party venue he was left astonished, for a brief moment he just couldn't help, but forget about his present ordeal and savor the moment. It was one hell of a scene, one which he had never seen before. The brightly colored disco lights, the loud blare of the music, the numerous boys and girls partying and swaying their body in symphony to the music. Well, to him this was simply phenomenal and he wondered why his parents never brought him to places like this other than the same old Trish Café where he regularly got ice cream, pizza, and some soft drinks.

Before long, he located Richmond. He was one of the bullies whom he had spent detention hours within school although he wasn't the one who invited him. It was Billy; Billy was more or less the leader of the bad boys' gang in school. Richmond took Foden to where Billy was seated. He was feeling like a demigod being surrounded by ladies of various sizes and height; all aesthetically pleasing. Foden wished he could be like Billy at that instance. Ah, Foden! I never knew you would be able to make it Billy said embracing Foden with open arms. He couldn't help but notice the voluminous bag Foden came along with. C'mon bro, this isn't some classroom stuff you know, this is a party. You've got to have fun and party to the fullest. Billy took the bag off Foden and tossed it aside.

Although he had not gone partying before, it didn't take long before Foden found his dancing shoes. He danced and swayed his body like never before. His energy seems to intensify with every new song the DJ blares through his deafening loudspeakers. Foden somehow managed to find himself on a bed in a poorly lit room. Of course, this couldn't be his room in Mr. Adams's house. Hey yo! Are you awake? A hoarse voice that seemed like that of Richmond drew his attention to the other side of the room. Indeed, it was Richmond who was lying rather haggardly on a sofa. It took some time for Foden to get back to his right senses. He asked Richmond where he was, where his bag was, how he got to where he was. Numerous questions flew out of his mouth in quick succession which Richmond never answered any as he was interrupted as he was about to speak by Billy and two other fierce looking boys who walked into the room.

Foden had his heart in his mouth, where exactly was he, what happened at the party and what on earth is Billy doing with a gun? The last question sent cold shivers down his spine as he struggled to understand what exactly was going on around him. Billy noticed his uneasiness and approached him. With a pat on his back, Billy assured him of his safety. Foden was slowly integrated into the fold and he ended up with other boys and girls who have left their homes both willingly and unwillingly.

Foden gradually became a chronic drinker, chain smoker, an armed robber who was adept in any form of negative social vices you can possibly think of. He dropped out of school, he lost everything he had – his happy family. However, he found a new family in Billy's gang who was willing to watch his back anytime, anywhere. The gang grew so strong in strength and decided to go rob a bank. The idea was initiated by Richmond who felt the gang needed to increase their income and have a better life. Since they were all forsaken at some point by those they treasured, the gang unanimously decided to make this robbery a reality.

The Place of Greatest Comfort

Welcome your breath as you find your relaxed state of mind and body.

Let your energy flow freely into your choice to let go, lie down, take comfort, and find solitude in the night hours, or before a long rest.

Prepare your body, your thoughts, your emotions, to fall forward into relief and inner comfort.

Let your soul feel prepared to feel held warmly by loving energy and inner light.

Take a few deep breaths in and exhales out to align with your comfort.

Help your body feel snuggled in and at peace.

Find all of the soft cushions and blankets you need to feel at home and at peace.

You are going to become more and more relaxed with every breath you take.

With every inhale, refresh your body with new oxygen, new energy, cleansing, and purifying your inner world.

With every exhale, release all of the tension from your body and your thoughts.

Release your worries and concerns.

Breathe in comfort, peace of mind, serenity.

Breathe out stress and worry, negativity, and pain.

As you connect further to your relaxed state of mind, feel soothed and nurtured by your choice to take time for a bedtime story.

Acknowledge that you are taking good care of yourself right now, at this moment.

Acknowledge that you are nurturing yourself back to health and giving yourself space to heal and rejuvenate.

Going deeper into this restful state, connect to your warmest memories of home, your most filling spaces you've known.

Connect to your places of greatest comfort in your mind and start to see in your third eye what that space looks like.

Open your heart and your mind to the part of your wholeness that feels the safest, the most comfortable, the most nurtured.

It could be your childhood home, or perhaps the space you live in now.

Maybe it is a beloved holiday memory or a film that gives you comfort.

It may be as simple as a picture in your mind of an old country cottage with a crackling fire and a pot of stew simmering on the stove.

Let your mind form this place of greatest comfort.

Take a few moments, breathing in slowly, letting it out steadily, and picture this serene and wholesome place...

You are here to find solace and inner harmony.

This dwelling space you are in that feels comforting to you is where you have come to feel at ease.

This is where you can become well again, nurtured, warmed by the fire.

This is where you will be fed by loved ones, family friends, or even your spiritual guides who have come to hold space for you.

When you take a look around this space, who is here to give you comfort?

What energies have come to support you and keep you safe and warm?

It can be anyone.

It can be anything.

Let your subconscious mind welcome whatever comes to give you balance and inner peace...

Continue to lay in this space, snuggled into your warm blankets, cozy and comforted as you welcome these energies, whether they are people or spirits.

What does it feel like to be surrounded by a warm, loving company?

How does it feel to have a place just to lay down and be taken care of?

You have no obligations here, no one to take care of.

You are the one being cared for.

You are the one who is being nurtured and loved.

Let the spirits and people who have traveled to this place in your heart gather around you and give you love and attention.

Feel their soft, friendly smiles giving you comfort and openness in your soul and mind.

As you continue to rest in the space of great comfort, the people, friends, allies, spirit guides, or others who have come to nurture and care for you are beginning to prepare a feast of the most nutritious and nourishing food.

All of your favorite foods that will heal you and make you feel whole are there.

You can hear the sound of foods being chopped, the sound of boiling soup on the stove, the aroma of fresh ingredients.

They are here to help you feel well and loved.

They are roasting things in the oven, the smell filling the whole space.

They are stirring the logs on the fire and making sure your blankets are tucked in.

Keeping you warm and cozy.

You have everything you need here.

You can just be.

You are being taken care of and loved in this place of greatest comfort.

The feeling that surrounds you is that of being held by all of the things that make you feel warm, whole, heart-felt, and secure.

The foods that are being prepared are the ones that make you feel nurtured and nourished.

The pleasantness of this place is what feels so healing and good.

It is your inner home and that good feeling that comes from your wholeness within.

As you are laying there, swaddled in blankets, taking in the aroma of your favorite dishes being prepared and the sounds of laughter and loving energy coming from those who have gathered, you feel someone lift you up and carry you, wrapped in warmth, to a table where there are many places laid for you and all of your company to share a delicious meal by a warm, glowing fire.

As you look from one end of the table to the other, it feels endless.

The candles are lit.

There is food on every inch of the table: fresh-baked bread, still hot from the oven, bowls of fresh fruits and herbs, homemade cookies, goblets of delicious drinks, roasted dishes, everything your heart desires, laid out in front of you.

You are surrounded by the love and affection of whoever is here with you.

The fire is crackling, and someone adds another log to keep it going.

As you look around the table at the feast, at your family and friends, your spiritual guides, you are filled with a sense of warmth and wonder.

There is nothing but kindness and generosity here, and you have no other concerns.

Everyone is merry and filling up on the wonderfully nutritious and nourishing foods.

You feel at peace, connected to this moment, to these friends and allies, to this meal.

When you have finished eating, and you glance around the table, you can sense and feel the contentedness of those around you, and it fills your heart with joy and tenderness.

You are warm in your blankets, full of the glorious feast, and held by the family that surrounds you.

You are free just to relax and breathe for a few moments, taking in this feeling of true peace and serenity.

Just as you feel like you could drift off to sleep, you feel someone lift you up again and carry you over to a soft, cushioned sofa near the fire.

You are tucked gently into your blankets, swaddled like a baby as the others gather around the sitting place near the fire.

Everyone is together for a delightful story to help everyone drift off into a safe and comfortable world of dreams.

You listen to the story as it begins.

Nothing feels more pleasant than having this comfort, this warmth, this generosity of spirit.

You can sense the blissfulness of everyone gathering together for a story to continue relaxing and feeling connected to the place of greatest comfort.

Your breath is slow and steady and deep.

You have nothing to think about or control in this place.

You have nothing to worry about, no problems to solve.

You are free just to relax and exist in the warmth of this space with these loving energies holding and embracing you.

As the story begins to unfold, you feel a release from deep within that lets you know that you are free to fall asleep anytime you feel like it.

You are welcome to listen until your body and mind float away, deeper and deeper into the world of dreams, into total relaxation and healing.

The story begins to take shape in your ears as you snuggle tightly into your covers, surrounded by the warm, healing light of the fire and the sense that you are not alone, that you are protected by those that surround you.

It begins as you take a deep breath in and sigh it out with relief...

Once upon a time, there was a cottage nestled deep in a forest.

The forest was very old, and the trees had been listening to all of the life within the forest for thousands of years.

The cottage had been there for a long time too, and tonight it was full of love and warmth and serenity.

The people inside of the cottage were baking loaves of bread and sweets, stirring a large pot of stew, and feasting on the delicious flavors of the Autumn time as the nights grew colder and the wind blew harder, whispering of the winter to come.

The feast was fragrant and sumptuous.

The taste of every bite was fulfilling.

Every nibble of soft, warm bread felt soothing to the soul; every sip of hot broth was warming to the heart.

The candles burned and the warm glow of firelight permeated to simple cottage walls, giving peace and comfort to all who sat at the table.

All around, there was laughter and kindness and friendship.

All around, there was life and beauty, and harmony.

The people sitting at the table felt satiated and at peace.

It was that time when all the food has been eaten and all the bellies are full when the gathering of life finds the comfort of a story to close the night.

When the feast was finished, the people gathered around the fire, along with all of the animals that were there to be peaceful and warm and gentle in front of the fire.

Someone began to tell a story, as everyone covered themselves in warm blankets, full of food at the feast's end...

The storyteller gathered their voice and came to a spot by the fire, and in soft, gentle, soothing tones began to tell a story that would send everyone off into a dream, and the story went something like this...

Once upon a time, there was a place of greatest comfort.

And no matter where you are in this world, you can find it.

All you have to do is close your eyes, take a nice deep breath, and remember this place that you know in your heart.

It is the place where the feat is always being made, where the fire is always warm, where the friends are always close by to wrap you in their arms and soothe you into a loving slumber.

This place is ancient and old, and yet it is fresh and new.

You have seen it in your dreams and in your daytime, too.

It is everywhere and nowhere; it is always by your side.

It is within your very nature, this story of heart and mind.

This place of greatest comfort is the story you will tell, every night when you go to sleep and find the place that suits you well.

This story is ongoing and will take you very far, deep into your dreamworld, to the farthest star.

Just gaze into the fire and hear the words unfold.

This is the place of greatest comfort, the greatest story ever told.

The whole world knows this story for we all have it in our hearts, to find our inner peace in a cottage safe at night.

All around the forest, deep to the river's edge, down below the valley, in every cave, behind every rock, along the highest ledge, all the creatures are resting and feeling comfort under the night sky.

There is a community in the nighttime, and family of night.

There are always those around you, falling deeper into sleep- every animal, every bird, all of the people around you by the fire who hear the story in the place of greatest comfort.

The story drifts away from you as you ink deeper into relaxation and calm.

You have never felt so comfortable, so take care of, so whole.

The words from the story are faint and distant now.

You can hear it through your quiet mind as you breathe in deeply and feel the sublime joy of rest and comfort tonight.

You sink even more deeply into the blankets and the cushions as the storyteller's voice become a part of your dream.

You are fully relaxed now and can let go of everything.

There is only this place for you now, this place of greatest comfort.

You are taken care of, loved, and held.

You are able to heal from this space, as you sleep, as you dream.

Your place of greatest comfort is always here for you and will always keep you safe and warm and protected as you trust your mind and body to fully release and relax, deep into your slumber.

Goodnight...sweet dreams...may your story continue tomorrow.

The Ship and The Sea

You are on your way to a sacred island, and the only way there is by ship.

Your journey will take time and feel soothing as you connect to the rhythm and embrace of the ocean waves.

You will begin your journey through your breath.

Your breath will help you release anything you may be holding onto at this time—anything from your day, your week…

You will start to feel your body relaxing more as you inhale and exhale, letting all of your cares and worries slip away from you.

Wherever you find tension in your body, let it release with your breath out.

Every breath lets you sink further into relaxation and comfort.

Inhale deeply, pulling fresh air into your muscles, your joints, and bones, your ligaments. Inhale into your organs and tissues.

Exhale any discomforts you may be holding onto.

Let them naturally relax out of you with your breath.

Enjoy the change in your body as you grow more relaxed with each new, refreshing breath cycle.

You will begin to feel heavier, sinking into your mattress or cushions more and more.

At the same time, you will feel lighter and freer, unshackled from pain and tension, anxiety, and stress...

Let your relief spill over and fill the room that surrounds you.

Let the energy of your peacefulness resonate and radiate into the atmosphere.

As you become lighter and freer, the heavier and more relaxed your body feels.

Fill the room with your serene position.

Begin to feel the surrounding room take a new shape and form as you continue your breath...

You are on a warm beach.

You hear a flock of seagulls cawing in the distance.

You can hear the constant churning of the sea, the waves rolling luxuriously over themselves, breaking into white foam on the west shore.

You are laying in the sand, and it feels perfectly warm on your body.

The sand is soft and dry where you are, and you are soothed by the temperature and the texture of the sand as you listen to the white-noise rhythm of the sea...

Here on this beach, you are perfectly still.

The sun's rays are at just the right temperature to feel relaxing and healing.

The light behind your eyelids is a soft, warm peachy-orange hue, from the sunlight hitting the skin of your face.

You can feel the hairs on your arm wave quietly in a gentle breeze, sending refreshing vibrations through your body...

The ocean is endless and vast.

You can feel its majesty from where you are lying, several meters away from the rolling surf.

The passion of the roaring sea is calling to you, asking you to traverse it with your courage and your love of adventure.

You sit up and look around at the beach, the shore, the twinkling diamond-light that shimmers on the water's surface...

On the horizon, you see a ship.

This ship is made of iron and wood.

It is the ship that has carried you far in life.

It has taken you everywhere you have wanted or needed to go.

This ship is, here again, to take you forward on your path of inner healing and relief.

You will find yourself feeling very drawn to this ship, feeling the urge to climb back on board, and take your next journey to heal the soul...

Standing up, you walk across the sand and feel it transform under your feet: from soft and dry, to damp, to wet as you get closer to the ocean waves.

Standing barefoot on this soothing wet sand, you wait for the tide to return and wrap around your ankles.

As the seawater pushes toward you, you feel a rise in your excitement, anticipating the feeling of water cresting your skin...

As the waves curl around your ankles and feet you notice how warm the water feels.

It is soothing, warm, refreshing, and clear.

It feels powerful against your skin and helps you to feel alive to your deeper truth and inner knowing.

You have all of your worries and cares to let go of, and the water in the waves begins to absorb all of the negative thoughts or feelings that you carry with you...

You are able to feel refreshed now, as the tide pulls away from you like a steady exhale from your lungs.

The tide takes away any feelings that you have right now that you want to let go of and release.

As the water pulls out and away, ebbing as an exhale, another flowing wave is coming back in to wash away any of your feelings of uncertainty or fear, any feelings of concern or worry...

Your feeling lighter and freer.

Your body is warm and relaxed in the sun and the water.

You are being relieved of your stress here at this moment.

Connect to your breath along with the ocean tide in your mind and let go of what wants to be set free and released...

...

You are ready to follow your journey forward now.

You are ready to make your journey to the ship so that you can set sail and find your deepest relaxation.

The ship is a great distance from you, and you will have to find your way there.

You are able to grow a fishtail and swim.

When you enter the seawater fully, you give your body to the energy of the ocean and of the water...

You become like a merman or merwoman, a human fish who swims with the dolphins and whales and finds great comfort in the warm, salty surface of the water.

Stepping fully into the water, you feel your tail form and propel you forward.

You are swimming close to the surface to feel the sun's rays on your body.

You can see the diamond twinkle of the sun reflecting on the water as you gain speed with your fins...

You feel the water gliding across your skin.

You are able to easily roll around in the water like a dolphin or a seal, playfully swimming and streaking through the water with joy.

Your body feels smooth and alive, fresh and clean as you go through the water, gaining speed and feeling light as air.

As you continue your trajectory toward the ship, you notice a pod of dolphins to either side of you as you swim.

They are jumping out of the water and arching through the air by your side, encouraging your journey forward, cheering you on as they swim alongside you.

They are with you all the way to your ship, your protectors in the sea, your escorts in the water...

You are nearing your ship, and as you get closer, you begin to realize just how massive it is.

This is the boat of your inner mind that takes you through your thoughts and dreams, your emotions, and your beliefs.

This ship helps you find your path, your goals, your fantasies, and your desires.

This ship was made for you alone and only you can steer the helm...

The ship is now within your grasp.

You swim right up to the side and note how ancient it looks, like an old-world cargo, or pirate ship, back in the days when you only used stars to find your way home...

It has seen many trips to many shores, and tonight is another journey.

You find a foothold and a ladder that leads up the side of the ship.

You are able to climb aboard this way, your fins and tail turning back into your regular limbs, lifting you up the ladder, one step at a time...

You are climbing over the rail and find yourself on deck.

You are the only one on board—the captain and the crew, and you only need yourself to take this journey.

You find your way to the helm of the ship so that you may steer it on course.

Where is your course going to take you?

Where does this ocean adventure lead?

With your hands gripping the wheel at the helm, you decide in your thoughts that you are ready to move forward.

Just as you think this thought, the ship pushes forward, slowly getting a move on, as if your thoughts were the wind that blew the sails.

You are in motion now.

Your ship is moving forward...

You are going farther out to sea now, where there is no land, where there is no one.

It is just you and the rocking ship of your dream world.

You can feel the wind lift the sails and put a breeze in your hair.

The sun is shining as you get farther from the shore.

You can look back now and see the spot on the beach where you were first beginning this journey.

You can see where you swam with the dolphins disappearing behind you as you steer further out.

The horizon is long and ageless.

It reaches out in all directions, curving around the Earth.

You are free here.

Alone, but not afraid.

Alone but not lonely.

Alone but full of love and light for your own path.

You are now surrounded by the ocean.

You are far out to sea, and the wind has pushed your ship far forward into serenity, peace, and calm.

Your feelings are free to expand here.

There is enough space for all of your thoughts and feelings, for all of your dreams and passions, for all of your intentions and needs...

This vast watery landscape holds the key to your openness with yourself. Underneath the surface lies all of your hidden truths.

You are going to find them slowly over time as you explore the realms of your unconscious on your ship of dreams.

There is nothing more sacred than to be at peace within yourself.

The waters of this ocean that you are sailing on are the waters of yourself.

You have nothing to hide or fear from yourself.

Everything that appears to you here that comes up for healing in this place is going to help you find your deeper truth, your deeper self-knowing, your relief...

Your ship is slowing now, and it is time to let the sails lay low as you are set adrift on the wide, open sea.

The breeze brings rhythm to the water's edge.

You feel that rhythm in the rocking of the ship, steady, long, slow, back and forth, bobbing grandly in the sun. It is a comforting rhythm.

It is subtle and deep. It is the vibration of light on water, with air from the wind and fire from the sun.

You are here to heal and renew.

You are here to refresh, and here the ocean revives your soul.

You can feel yourself being soothed by the rocking of the ship.

You listen to the water lapping up against the side of the ship, the sound of water on wood...

You feel focused, serene, peaceful.

You are free to just sit on the deck and watch the sunbeams turn into bright pinks and oranges, purples and lavenders, as the sun starts its descent into the water.

The bright red-orange sun becomes hot pink as it smears against the water's surface.

The water is colored now with the light of the setting sun...

You are here, reflecting the opening of your soul in this water.

This water waves with the frequency of your mind and your thoughts.

The gentle ripple of the ocean reflects your peacefulness and calmness.

You are as the water, ebbing and flowing, rocking and swaying, soothing and refreshing...

The power of this water fills your soul and lets you feel connected to your primal roots, your ancient wisdom, your sacred intuition.

The waterline is thick against the sides of your ship.

You feel perfectly safe and calm as the sun sizzles into the western horizon, and the stars come out to shine through the night...

In the soothing ocean night, you feel held by the quiet and peace of this place.

You are far away, listening to the water, hearing nothing but your own rhythm on the sea.

You feel embraced by your own journey and adventure into the deep unknown.

You feel refreshed to have all that you are right inside of you...always...

You feel the starlight on your skin.

They are the only lights for hundreds of miles in all directions.

You look up at the stars and then down at the ocean water.

There is a perfect, crystal clear reflection of the starry night sky on the surface of the water.

As far as the eye can see, in all directions, from horizon to horizon, above and below, there are stars.

The stars of the water are a mirror image of the stars in the sky.

It is like floating through a sea of stars, like floating through space, far from the surface of the Earth...

You feel like you have been here before, in this starry expanse, like you could really be floating far out in the cosmos.

Then, you hear the lapping of the water, and you remember your ship is with you, holding you, taking you forward on your journey, and wherever it is going to lead you, far off in your dreams and sleep...

The starlight surrounding you, from the sky and the water below, fill your heart and mind with soothing relief.

You are safe and content to just be here on the deck of this ship.

The air is warm.

The rhythm of the ship is rocking you gently, back and forth...back and forth...back and forth...

You are at peace now, in your body, in your mind, in your heart.

You have all that you need to feel at ease, far away in the starry night of the ocean.

Your ship is carrying you to your dreams now, and you can feel the boat push forward, wind, in the sails as you lie in comfort on the deck under the stars.

Your ship knows where to go and will deliver you to your dreamscape as you sail farther and farther off into the horizon...

Your dreams will come as the sun rises in the East.

You will begin to find the place in your subconscious thoughts where your ship of dreams wants to take you tonight.

You will find everything you need there.

All you have to do now is just rest here.

Let your ship take you forward.

Let the soothing sway of the boat rock you gently on your journey tonight...

Feel the light of the stars turning pink with morning's promise as you drift farther and farther into dreamland...

Your ship will carry you there...just breathe.

The Hot Air Balloon Ride

Sometimes, all you need is to feel far from all of your cares and worries.

Sometimes, all you need is to glide through life on a serene cloud, floating across a pale blue sky.

If you have ever been on an airplane ride and looked out the window, then you have probably noticed the ethereal world above the clouds.

It is so calm and relaxing, high off the ground, and far away from all of the stress of life.

Have you ever taken a ride in a hot air balloon?

Have you ever been lifted off the ground slowly, like you were being carried by a gentle giant to a restful place?

Your journey into peacefulness and relaxation will begin on the ground, preparing for your journey of slow and tender flight, as you crawl slowly through the clouds in a comfortable basket.

Begin your ascent first by lying down in a comfortable position.

If your body needs to be adjusted at all to help you for the most comfort in this space, make those adjustments now before you enter a place of total stillness.

You are going to be carried away on the air, firstly through your breath.

Your breath will align you with your inner harmony and balance.

Your breath will help fill you with the peacefulness you desire and help you release all of the cares and worries you may be carrying around with you right now.

Every inhales is a beautiful source [of comfort, refreshment, and light.

Every exhale is a letting go, a release of tension, a movement closer to restful relaxation.

Breathe here for a few moments.

Connect to your body.

Connect to your feelings.

Connect to the sense of relief from your breath...

You are here to feel free from the world of deadlines and agendas.

You are here to only exist within yourself and your deeper sense of true peace and balance.

This practice of connecting to your physical body through your breath, and your spiritual essence through your creative mind, is what will help you to refresh your life-force energy and feel fully healed, refreshed, and connected to your inner soul.

Your only purpose now is just to float through a heavenly landscape.

Underneath your body, you begin to feel the softness of grass on a majestic hillside.

It is a bright and beautiful, sunny day.

As you look up into the sky, you can see that it is full of the most glorious, puffy, white clouds.

You are going to feel those clouds soon, gliding through and above them with the magic of your higher consciousness.

The soft grass around you is yielding, comforting, and pleasurable on your skin.

The warm sunlight feels just right and the very subtle, gentle breeze is just right...for a hot air balloon ride...

You look over now and see the basket just walking distance away—the basket that will carry you far off into the heavens.

You are eager to go over to it and witness the gigantic balloon rise up off the ground, full of the hot air that will lift you up.

The basket is easy for you to climb into a much larger than you would have thought.

There is enough room inside for you to lie down in any direction.

The balloon is airing up while you are climbing inside.

It is starting to lift off of the grassy earth and align with the basket, to float over and hover above it.

You can feel yourself feeling elated but calm—excited, but relaxed.

Your path is up and up and up, and there is no other landscape, but the clouds on high.

You will get there soon.

Your balloon is almost ready to lift you up and all you have to do when the time comes is pull on the cord to send you off the ground.

Inhale deeply, slowly pulling fresh air into your lungs...and exhale gently out.

Again, inhale slowly and steadily, gathering all of the hot air you will need to soar high up in the clouds...and exhale.

Breathe out all of the cares and worries that will weigh you down.

Breathe away all of the tension that will keep your balloon on the ground...

You are ready, and your balloon is ready.

It's time to pull the cord and feel your ascent.

The cord is easy to pull.

It feels effortless as you give it a tug and release hot air into the giant balloon above your head.

With one tug, you begin to feel your body in the basket, hover off the ground.

You pull the cord again and feel an even bigger lift off the grass.

You are now fully off the surface of the Earth with just a couple of tugs...

You can feel the pull upward. It is smooth and slow.

Your hot air balloon can only go about 2 miles per hour.

There will be no speed on your journey.

You can take all the time you need to just feel pulled upward by the balloon and watch the world around you transform as you are carried higher and higher above the ground...

Your path is taking you further up.

The world below you become smaller as you ascend at a snail's pace.

You look off to the east, and you see a river flowing smoothly.

You think to yourself how big it seems when you are standing right beside it, and how small it seems now that you are floating high above it...

The river is full of life, and it flows smoothly, cutting across the land as far as the eye can see, the sunlight of the day glistening on its surface.

The river becomes smaller and smaller as you float higher and higher, taking a deep breath in and exhaling gently...

You look to the west, and you see a great, wide forest that pushes far across the land.

The trees seem infinite, endless.

As you glide high above the trees, you feel like you can hear the rustle of every squirrel, every bird, every forest creature rummaging for food.

There is no space between the horizon and the trees.

It stretches on forever...

The higher you go, the smaller the trees become, the wood of the branches and trunks disappearing behind the green foliage.

The tops of the trees, which once seemed so close, are now at a great distance from your hot air balloon.

You can feel the journey getting steadily closer to the clouds...

You look out of the basket to the south, and you see fields and meadows reaching far across the land, sewing a patchwork quilt of land as far as your eye can see to the south.

The lands of the farmers, the cattle, the goats, and the sheep—the land of food that grows, of harvests, and abundance from the fertile soil.

This land will stretch out for miles more, as your balloon gets ever higher, and can see that much farther across the land.

You look out to the north and are much higher now.

You begin to see the curve of the Earth from this height and feel completely restful as you look to the north star, already visible from this height in the sky.

You have ascended to the atmosphere of the cloud world, and it is here that you will find your greatest peacefulness and comfort.

It is here that you can let all of your worries and cares drift off and away from you, falling back to the earth as you drift through the clouds...

Look around you as you inhale deeply and exhale smoothly.

You are completely surrounded by puffs of white moisture.

They look like giant cotton balls piled together in beautiful mounds of softness.

You can no longer see the surface of the earth.

You are too high above the clouds now and can only see a great plain of white in every direction you face...

Your basket is moving slowly, but you feel the momentum of your balloon as it wafts on the breeze of the high atmosphere.

You have no trouble breathing here.

You can take deep, fulfilling breaths.

You can feel totally relaxed as you inhale and exhale from this point in the sky...

Breathe now as you let in the magnificent scenery of an all-white horizon fill your soul.

Breathe into this place of total calm and serenity.

Let the clouds high above the earth; comfort you.

You are warm here.

You are safe.

You have enough oxygen to breathe.

All you have to do is take in the majesty of this place.

The whole world above the clouds looks like a tundra of snow and ice for thousands of miles.

It looks angelic and full of bright light, the light from the sun reflecting off of the cloud faces.

Beneath the clouds is the whole landscape of the world you know—the world where you eat, sleep, work, love...

This place high above the earth, beyond the clouds, is where you can come to be to feel refreshed, relaxed, a sense of internal peace, and quiet.

You are not going to need any of your worries and fears up here.

All of your doubts, complaints about your daily life or work life, anything that is causing you stress, can be released from this hot air balloon ride...

Take a moment to consider this: what are you worried about today?

What has been causing you stress or discomfort?

Can you name it?

Can you make it specific?

What is the one thing that has been on your mind of late?

Let it come fully into your thoughts.

As you let it take shape in your thoughts, turn it into something you can hold in your hand, a physical object that represents this worry or stress...

It could be a heavy bag of sand that represents the weight that you feel from your work or your home life.

It could be a dollhouse to symbolize how you feel about your home or your living space.

It could be a person that has been upsetting you or weighing you down. Anything is possible from this place within your mind.

Do not judge yourself for how it comes up or how it forms.

Simply allow it to take shape so that you can hold it in your hands...

Notice the clouds again and the atmosphere you are floating again.

Reminding yourself of your stress may have brought up those feelings for you again.

Look out to the clouds.

You are here in a hot air balloon, free to just release the pain you are suffering, free to align with your highest consciousness and internal vibration of light...

Here you are, high above the clouds, facing your current anxiety or worry.

You are holding it in your hands, and you are ready to let it go.

You can hold it over the side of the balloon and prepare to let it go.

You are not hurting it, whatever it is.

It is a symbolic release of what has been holding you back from your relaxation and relief.

It is a symbolic action to cut the cords with your tension, worry, and doubt...

Hold the symbolic object over the edge and promise to let go of everything right here, right now.

You have no reason to hold onto this part of your life anymore.

You have no reason to doubt yourself.

You have no reason to fear to let go of this issue or these fears.

It is time.

Here, high above the clouds, it is time for you to say farewell to this part of your life.

It serves no purpose.

It only causes distress and discomfort.

Let it go.

Let it fall far away, through the clouds to wherever it must go.

Resolve to know that you are free of it.

Release it fully and take a nice, long breath in through your nose.

Hold your breath here for a moment, like you were holding the object over the side of the basket...and release the breath, letting it flow away from you.

Notice the serene landscape around you, unfolding as far as your eye can see...

You are safe here.

You are free.

You have released your discomfort.

You can now relax a little more and let yourself delve more deeply into your unconscious thoughts and dreams.

Here in the heavens, high above the soft, cotton-like clouds, you can prepare for your ascent farther and deeper into dreamland.

You will not return to the Earth tonight.

Tonight, you will continue to float high above the ground in your hot air balloon and find all of the relief you have been looking for.

Perhaps you have another object you want to release and toss over the side of the basket.

You can do that now.

You can take a moment to reflect on whatever happens to come up for healing.

Let it take shape and form in your mind.

Let it become something you can hold in your hands so that you can fully release it into the atmosphere, cutting ties with whatever has been weighing you down...

As you take a moment to do this, continue with your soothing breath, high up in the clouds.

Don't let go of the landscape that has been giving you so much comfort.

You are safe here.

You cannot fall.

You cannot be harmed.

You can breathe easily here.

You will find all of the relief you need simply by existing in this place high above the Earth.

The total calm and serenity of this world is what calms you and puts your heart at ease.

It is the place that prepares you for your dreams tonight.

It is the place that calls you home to your most comfortable and relaxed body, mind, and spirit.

You have everything you need now.

You are free to drift off, farther and farther into the clouds...farther and farther into your subconscious thoughts...farther and farther into the great beyond...the land of your dreams...

Float away...high on the clouds...float away... with your breath slow and steady...float away...with your heart full of peace...sweet dreams...

A Walk Through the Clearing

"I don't know how long I had been walking for, but I was sure that I must be almost there. My friend said it would take an hour or so to get to the clearing, but I had budgeted for two hours because I knew I wanted to take my time walking. I hadn't brought a watch with me but judging by how far the sun had moved since I started, I was sure it had been nearly two hours at this point. I felt the crunching of the gravel under my feet as I continued to follow the marked trail and took my time in admiring the sights around me. Luscious greenery adorned the path on either side and every now and again, I would see a squirrel or a bird flutter away from the path and into the trees to avoid being seen by me. Of course, I would always pause and watch, enjoying the experience of being alone in the forest with these beautiful creatures.

As I continued walking, I could see the path beginning to widen up ahead. In the distance, I could hear the gentle rushing of water and I knew that I had arrived where I was meant to. Despite how excited I was, I slowed my pace, even more, wanting to take in all of the sights that were arising before me. After a long, hard year of going through many of life's trials and tribulations, this was my first true break alone and I did not want to waste it worrying or drowning in the overwhelm of my reality. I paused for a moment and breathed in deeply, smelling the green air from the fresh forestry around me. I sighed, feeling the sun shining against my back as it continued to rise through the sky. It must have been around 11:30 AM, as I had hit the trail around 9:30 AM. The heat of the sun was beginning to grow warmer and the forest was slowly drying out for the day as the dew from the night before began to evaporate. I took another step forward, and then another, allowing the lull of the waterfall's sweet sound to draw me forward. As I did, the view of the clearing began to open in front of me.

The clearing was just as my friend had described it: there was a large grassy patch with a crystal-clear body of water off to the right side. The trees grew around the edges of the grass, yet not too close to the waterfall. There was plenty of space to enjoy the view or get into the waterfall should I desire. Around the edges of the waterfall, the trees rose high, although none were taller than the peak of the waterfall itself. The waterfall fell down from a sheer cliff, which clearly had trees lining the falling body of water on either side at the top as well. The clearing felt cozy, almost like a small den that had been carved out of the vast forest.

I walked closer to the waterfall, and as I did, I could see the frothy bubbles foaming around the water from where the waterfall was rushing into it. As I reached the water, I noticed footprints were still formed in the sand at the edges of the water from people who had been there recently and I felt a sense of comfort in knowing that this space was enjoyed by many. I, too, slipped my own shoes off and followed the footprints, walking around the edge of the water and finding myself next to the cliff, looking in behind the waterfall itself. There, a moist rock wall that had been smoothed by the moving water stood tall and strong. I admired the way the water looked and wondered if anyone had ever crawled in there before to see the water from the back. I gazed at the trail that may lead there but decided against it as I worried it may be too difficult for me to do on my own and knew that I was alone so if I needed help I would be in trouble. After a few more moments, I turned around and saw the lush green grass behind me and gazed out into the clearing from the opposite angle from where I had walked in from. I followed my footprints back toward my shoes, taking my time and feeling the moist ground beneath my feet. The sun continued to shine down over the clearing, and I could feel it growing warmer with every passing moment.

When I reached my shoes again, I turned back toward the water and began breathing in deeply and exhaling all of my breath as much as I could. I sat down and dipped my toes into the edge of the water, feeling how cool it was against my skin, and meditating on the sensation of peace that was wrapped all around me. As I looked into the water, I could not help but notice how grateful I was for some clarity in my life, even if that clarity was merely the clear water at the edge of the waterfall. I looked up into the waterfall itself and saw how the water was white with fury from rushing off the edge of the cliff so fast and paused for a moment to reflect on the lesson before me. That was, no matter how chaotic things may get, and no matter how fast, hard, or long we may fall for, there is always the potential that we may end up resting at the edge of calmness after our journey. I realized there was no reason for me to hold so tightly to my stresses and worries when I could just as easily relax into the moment and trust that in the end, I could find my calmness once more.

Falling for Her

Daisy lived up the street in her father's farmhouse where she often worked early in the morning feeding the chickens, milking the cows, and rounding up the farm boys to put them to work for the day. After she was done, she would head to the bus stop and await the bus to take her to school. Rusty lived out of the way a bit, in a trailer park where his father had raised him since his Mom left them when they were younger. He was a rugged boy with a heart of gold, although he didn't show his heart to many for fear of what could happen if people saw him as sensitive instead of strong. Each morning, Daisy would get on the bus and Rusty would have a seat casually available for her, and she would always sit next to him. They didn't talk much at school as Rusty was a year ahead, but each morning they would talk endlessly on the bus about their wonders and curiosities, often landing on questions about what life outside of their small farm town would be like. Rusty was eager to leave it all behind and start fresh, and Daisy wondered what it would be like, although she had hesitations.

When Rusty graduated, he talked at great length about leaving, yet he never actually did. Instead, he took a job at Daisy's Dad's farm and worked there for a year while Daisy continued going to school to graduate. Each morning, Rusty would arrive at the farm and the two would feed the chickens, milk the cows, and prepare the daily task lists for the rest of the workers. Rusty would then work through the day as Daisy went to school, and he would greet her when she got home. When his work was done, Daisy would always come out to say goodbye and then Rusty would leave for the evening.

After a year of doing this, Daisy finally graduated and Rusty was eager to get out of town. The two had been talking in great length about what they would do, yet they had never fully settled on a plan. Rusty wanted to move to Chicago, but Daisy was not ready to leave Oklahoma. Over time, Rusty worried that he may have to move away and leave Daisy behind. It was around this time that Rusty realized that he had fallen deeply in love with Daisy, as he could not imagine leaving her behind and living a life without her. Daisy had not said anything, but she, too, was terrified of Rusty leaving and forgetting about her as she had also fallen in love with Rusty. Still, the two could not decide what it was that they wanted to do.

When the day came that Daisy graduated, Rusty came to her graduation and stood off in the distance so Daisy's father wouldn't see him there. Daisy got excited upon seeing Rusty there, and immediately after the ceremony rushed over to see him. To her surprise, Rusty wrapped his arms around her, kissed her forehead, and congratulated her for graduating. He spun her around in a circle, cheering for her and enjoying this moment of finally getting to hold her close. They both felt the depth of their love growing as they embodied this moment together. When they were done, Daisy went back to see her family and celebrated with them at a local diner before heading back to the farm.

The next day, Rusty arrived at the farm, only this time his car was packed full of his belongings. Daisy's heart sank as she realized what was happening, so she stayed in the house, as she did not want to have to say goodbye. She watched out the window as Rusty talked to her father and let him know it was time for him to go, and Daisy's father shook Rusty's hand. Rusty then looked toward the house and caught a glimpse of Daisy in the window. He waved to her to come out, but Daisy was sad and instead sat down at the kitchen table and stirred a spoonful of sugar into her tea. Rusty came into the house, much to her surprise, and asked Daisy to go with him to Chicago and live their lives together, like he knew they were meant to do. Daisy frowned and said she could not leave her family, especially without knowing when she would be able to see them again. Rusty had it all figured out, though, as he dropped an envelope on the table in front of her. "That's enough money for you to buy a bus ticket home if you decide you don't want to be with me in Chicago anymore, and I'll bring you back here every other month for a visit, I promise. Will you come?" Rusty asked. Daisy smiled, picked up the envelope, and decided she would give it a try.

Years went by and Daisy and Rusty continued living in Chicago and visiting their families in Oklahoma every other month. Daisy never used the bus fare to return home, but eventually, she did use it to buy a new cradle for their firstborn baby. Together, Daisy and Rusty raised a family of three children, two cats, and a dog in their home in Chicago. They spent each day talking about the wonders of the world, reminiscing on their days at the farm, and enjoying each other's company.

One day, Daisy's father died and he had left his farm behind for Daisy to keep. Together, Daisy and Rusty decided to relocate their family back to the old farm where they picked up where they had left off years before as if they had never skipped a beat. Their kids took the bus to school, and on that bus, their eldest daughter Rosie fell in love with a boy named Evan from the trailer park up the road. Daisy and Rusty often smiled as they looked out at their kids boarding the bus, recalling the days when they themselves were just teenagers falling in love.

College Sweethearts

When Carole and Jordon were freshmen in college, they met at a coffee cart outside of the main entrance to the old campus lot. Their meeting was like one straight out of a storybook, complete with cool fall weather, colorful leaves are strewn about, and cozy scarves, and toques adorning everyone to help them stay warm. One morning in the fall of freshman year, Carole was standing with her friends in line at the coffee cart and Jordon was working the cart to earn some extra cash to help purchase new filming equipment. When Carole was next in line, she walked up to the cart and ordered an Americano with extra whip cream. "Odd order," Jordon answered, scribbling it down on a piece of paper. "Whip cream on coffee?" He asked. "Just the way I like it." Carole smiled, handing Jordon exact change for her drink. As she handed him the change, Carole and Jordon locked eyes and smiled, pausing for a moment to take in the simple and sweet beauty of falling in love with each other.

Carole thought Jordon was attractive, so she made a mental note of which cart he was working at and came back to that cart each morning for weeks after. Some mornings, Jordon would be working and he would prepare her drink for her. Others, he would not be working but he would always seem to be nearby the cart so that when she was done ordering they could share some conversation before they each parted way to attend their respective classes. Without ever telling the other, the two of them always did their best to ensure that they would see each other every single morning.

Carole and Jordon grew fond of their morning conversations. They also started getting braver and braver as they each began leaving little hints about having an attraction toward the other. Carole would always smile and give Jordon a hug if he was not working, and Jordon would always draw little smiley faces or hearts on Carole's Americano with the whipped cream. These two lovers had a great deal of fun falling for each other and enjoy casually flirting with one another each morning before classes.

One day, during the middle of winter, when it was particularly cold outside, Jordon proposed that the two of them head inside and grab a bite to eat. It just so happened that Carole did not have to be in class for another forty-five minutes, so she agreed and the two of them walked together to the cafeteria hall to eat their breakfasts with each other. They spent the entire time laughing, enjoying each other's company, and falling even more deeply in love with each other.

When the breakfast was done, the two parted ways and went to their respective classes. All morning, they both found themselves distracted by thoughts of the other. They loved how it felt so normal to be with each other, and how spending time together seemed to come so easily. When their classes were over that day, Carole went back to her dorm to study. At some point that evening, she heard a knock at her door. When she answered it, she saw none other than Jordon standing there, smiling, with his hands stuffed in his pockets. He paused for a moment before asking if she wanted to go to the library with him to study together, and Carole happily agreed. The two of them spent the evening studying, joking, and enjoying each other's company.

After that, Carole and Jordon began hanging out almost daily. They would share breakfast, study sessions, or even just walks around the campus as they enjoyed each other's presence. When spring break came, they carpooled back to see their family as they both came from the same small town in Connecticut. They would listen to their favorite songs on the ride back home, sing, laugh and spend even more time getting to know each other along the way.

As the years went by, Carole and Jordon became inseparable. In sophomore year, they spent spring break on a vacation together in Cape Cod where they enjoyed delicious seafood dinners and beach walks together each evening. In junior year, they spent Christmas at each other's family's houses, enjoying two dinners, and sharing the opportunity to meet each other's extended families. By senior year, they fell so deeply in love that there was no way these two could be separated from each other's company.

When graduation was right around the corner, Jordon began acting strangely. Carole thought he was reconsidering their relationship since college would be over soon and became worried that the love of her life was preparing to leave her. Jordon became scared because he had no idea what the love of his life would think about him wanting to spend the rest of their lives together. Shortly after the two walked across the stage, Jordon got down on one knee and proposed to Carole. He proposed that she marry him, that they move in together, that they start their careers, and that they eventually have the children and dogs that they always dreamed about having during their late-night study sessions. Carole cried as she realized that Jordon had been acting weird because he was about to propose, not because he was preparing to leave her. She said yes, and the two cried together as they celebrated the reality that they would go on to live the rest of their lives together. The two lived happily ever after, as they say in the fairy tales.

The Peaceful Path

Gary was a forty-something-year-old man who had been working for the same office job for nearly twenty years now. He was a busy man with many meetings every day, bosses who had high expectations of him, and a family at home who regularly demanded more of his time and attention than he felt he had to give. Gary always strived to be everything his family, boss, and friends wanted and needed him to be, yet he never felt like he could keep up. Often, he would find himself standing in the shower at the beginning of what would be a very long day attempting to wash away his troubling thoughts. Gary felt like his mind was racing all the time, and sometimes in the shower was his only opportunity to clear his thoughts so that he could feel at peace with himself. It never lasted, but for those few moments in the shower in between thoughts of what he had to get done that day he would feel fleeting sensations of relief.

One day, Gary went to work and it became too much for him to handle. He was already feeling guilty about missing his Mom's birthday dinner because of needing to be at work, so when his boss started yelling at him, Gary couldn't take it anymore. He found himself in the bathroom with the door locked, talking himself out of a panic attack, and trying to find a moment of peace. He realized this was happening more and more: he would become overwhelmed with the demands of life and be desperate to feel even a fleeting moment of peace in between the stress. Despite how hard he wished for it, Gary could never seem to find the peace that he was looking for.

Gary searched everywhere for the peace he desired. He tried buying the things that he believed would bring him peace, but all they did was cause him to feel sad when it didn't work. He tried to create peace by purchasing expensive vacation packages for his family, but all he felt was stressed over the added expenses that he had to incur. He tried to talk to local yogis and meditation guides to try and find out how to get peace into his life, and while he understood the logic behind all of their teachings, Gary would not allow himself to actually do what the guides said. Instead, he would write off their suggestions as being "too easy" and then he would begin going about his life as usual.

Gary spent years upon years trying to find out how he could find peace, and eventually, he gave up. He became so fed up that the methods he was trying were not working that he decided peace must be an illusion and that everyone claiming to have it must be lying. Gary became so angry with all of the yogis and meditation guides in his town that any time he heard someone talk about them he would frown, claim that peace was a load of nonsense and that it was unattainable, and then end the conversation or leave.

One day, Gary became so angry with his failure to find peace and his deep-seated need for experiencing peace, that he threw his hands up in the air and admitted defeat. He was in his car after work, sitting in the grocery parking lot, and he was truly angry after being cussed out by his boss for the duration of the day. To put it simply, Gary was fed up with his life and he had reached the point where he could no longer take it. With his hands in the air, Gary yelled at the skies out of the front window of his car. "I can't take it anymore!" He shouted, dropping his fists into his lap and leaning his head over the steering wheel. "I can't take the stress, the demands, the overwhelm. I love my family and I can't even handle them anymore! It's too much!" He muttered, feeling his eyes flooding hot with tears. Now, this was a big deal for Gary. Gary was a very proud man, he was so proud that he rarely showed his anxiety, stress, or anger to anyone else. So, for Gary to be sobbing out all of his pent-up stress in his car was a big deal.

After several minutes of sobbing in his car and releasing the stress that he had been carrying around inside of him, Gary found that there were no tears left. Almost suddenly, he no longer had the fear of what he had been holding on inside of him anymore, there was no sadness or stress left to be experienced at that moment. Gary sat up, wiped his eyes, and looked around his car to make sure that no one had seen him lose it in the grocery store parking lot. When he realized he was alone, and that all of his emotions had been felt, Gary felt a surge of peace rush through him. Just like that, he found what he had been looking for all along. At that moment, Gary realized that peace was not something that he could buy, manufacture, or obtain. Instead, peace was emotion like any other, and it could be experienced and expressed through allowing himself to just be.

From that day forward, Gary made a routine of allowing himself private space to feel and express his emotions to himself. This way, he could continue to hold his pride around his family, without carrying the burden of his stress with him, too. As a result, Gary became a happier, healthier, and more peaceful man overall. He even joined a few of those meditation classes and followed some local yogi's through their practices as he learned to cultivate even more peace from within.

The Landlady

On the Quiet Afternoon train, Willy Weaver had been traveling down from London with a switch on his way to Swindon, and it was around 9 p.m. when he arrived at Bath, and the moon came up over the buildings across from the station entrance from an open starry sky. The water, though, was cold, and the breeze on her face was like a smooth ice knife. "Sorry," he said, "but isn't there a fairly cheap hotel too far from this place?" "Try the Bell and the Dragon, and it is just down this road," responded the porter. "You could have been checked in, but it was around a fourth of a mile on the other side of the road." Never before had he been to Bath. Nobody who worked there, he did not know. But Mr. Greenslade told him that it was a beautiful city at the head office in London. Willy was seventeen years old, and then he went and presented to the Director of Division as soon as you settled him. He added a new overcoat that was marine blue, a new trilby hat, and a jacket that were both brown and felt good and was walking the street briskly. Off late, this is the first thing he always wanted to do first. A common character trait possessed by a vast majority of successful businessmen was Briskness, he had decided.

The big shots are good at the headquarters. It was incredible. Only many large houses along each side, all alike, were not in this broad street. It was apparent that once they were costly houses. They had porches and columns, and four to five steps up to their windows. Yet now he could see even in the darkness that the paint on their doors and windows stripped from the woodwork and that the beautiful white facades were crackled and gritty by neglect. At that point, Willy observed a manually written message in one of the top sheets, in a window first floor brilliantly lit up by a road light that was not six yards away.

There was a container located beneath the notice which was full of pussy willows, high and dazzling. His development finished. He came a little closer. He drew nearer. Green anchors are holding the window tightly on both ends (some smooth material). The pussy willows looked lovely. The first thing he saw is a flame burning into a fire in the chest, he went up straight up and staring into space through windows. A sweet little dachshund rolled up on the rug in front of the fire and tucked its head into its stomach. The space itself was lined with fun furniture to the point that it could be seen in the half night.

There was a baby-sized piano, many plump arms, a massive parrot that was locked inside of a cage at the corner of the room, and a huge couch. In an environment like that, Willy assured himself that pets are usually a good sign; and in all, it seemed like a pretty fit house to live above. It would be more pleasant than The Bell and Dragon. A bar would be cozier than a boarding house on the other side. In the mornings there are drinks and games, and a lot of people are chatting with, and it's probably a bit cheaper too. A few nights ago, he had sat in a bar because he enjoyed it. Having never been to a boarding house, he was a little scared to be perfectly honest. The title itself evoked visions of watery rain, rapacious landladies, and a strong scent in the living room of kippers. Following two to three minutes of sitting like this in the snow, Willy wanted to go on and dig into The Bell and Dragon before he talked about it. He turned around. He turned around. And it happens to him a gay thing then. His eyes were captured and held peculiarly by the tiny note that was there, and he turned back and away from the door. It said, BED Or BREAKFAST. Everything resembled a goliath bruised eye, gazing at him through the glass and bolting him back, hauling him in, keeping him where he is and not to leave this house and what he knows first, really moving from window to the front entryway of the home, heading along the means paving the way to it and scanning for the ring. BED AND BREAKFAST, BED, AND BREAKFAST. He pushed the button. He hit it. He felt something ringing in the back room far from it, and it ought then to have been so soon because he did not have the time to open his hand, and a woman stood standing. You usually start by ringing the bell and waiting for at least thirty seconds to open the door. This woman, though, was like a jack in the box. He rang the sound, and she came out! She came out. He climbed it. She was about 45 or 50, and she offered him a warm welcome smile as soon as she saw him.

She replied politely, "Please come back." She got away, left the door open, and Willy immediately began going into the house. There were extraordinarily current expectations and, more precisely, the need to bring her into that house. He said, keeping himself off, "I saw the note in the door. "I wondered about a room."

"Everything is ready for you, my dear," she said. Her face was pink in color and round in shape, and her eyes were a very soft blue. Willy told her, "I've been en route to The Bell and Dragon. She asked," Why don't you come inside where it is warm and away from the cold?" "What fee do you charge?" "Fifty-six pence a night, plus coffee." It's been great, really easy, but you don't want to get a note from your door to catch the eye. He was willing to pay less than half of it. "If this is too much," she said, "maybe perhaps I could only shorten that little bit. Do you want an egg for breakfast? Eggs are pricey. It's sixpence less without the egg."

"I want to live here a bit," she said. "I wish that you would. Please come in." He seemed like the mother of her best friend, inviting him into the house for the celebrations of Christmas. Willy got his hat off the bridge and jumped over it. "So just," she said, "there was no other hat or dress in the room, and I would let you support you with your jacket." No colors and no sticks- none. There was no sun. He said, grinning at him on her arm as he went upstairs. "We have all this to us." "I'm not too often happy, you know, to welcome a stranger to my little house," Willy assured himself that the old girl is a bit dotty. But who is offering the fuck at five or six o'clock a night? He said kindly, "I should have assumed that candidates would swamp you. But the difficulty is that I'm still willing, spending 24 hours a day just sitting in this house only on the possibility out there, that a good youthful man will come. And it's so much fun, my love, such great joy if I come now and again, terrific. It's so much for me to talk to me. I'm just ready to say what I want. "Oh, my sweet, I am, of course, I am. "For you," she said, and Willy's blue eyes gradually roamed across his feet and then again. "It was like you," she said. At the landing on the new floor, she told him, "This floor is mine." She replied, "And it's all yours. She escorted him to a bedroom at the front that was small but lovely and switched the light on while she went in. "Then it's your room. I hope you love it." "Tomorrow morning's sun is coming into the door. It's Mr. Perkins, isn't it?" he replied, "Yes." "Weaver." "Mr. Weaver." Mr. Weaver. How lovely. To dry them out, Mr. Weaver, I have placed a water bottle between the plates. It's so easy to have a warm bottle of water that is in a clean bed, don't you agree? He realized the bedclothes were stripped off his bed and that on one side, the mattress-clothes were flipped gently sideways, all prepared for anyone to go. "I'm pleased you seemed to have come in," she said, earnestly gazing at her eyes. "I was beginning to worry." Bill replied, "It's fine," she said, "To be honest, I've been very grateful to see you. He put the bad that he was carrying on the bench and started opening it. "You managed to get anything to eat before you arrived here?" he said, "I do not feel hungry, but thank you for the offer."

"Somewhat great now. I'm going to leave you now so you can get it off. But before you go to sleep, would you be kind enough to go into the sitting-room on the ground to sign the Book? All of us have to do that because it's the law of the land, and we don't want anyone going to break. I guess I'll go to bed soon because tomorrow I have to get up very early to go to a job." So, Willy didn't stress in any event since his landowner appeared to be a little off her rocker. All factors put into consideration, in addition to the fact that she was guiltless—there wasn't any contention—yet she was additionally a sort and liberal soul. He thought she had most likely lost or had never gotten over a kid during the fight. So, he jogged down the stairs to the ground floor and went into the lounge a couple of moments later, in the wake of unloading his bags and washing his hands. Even if his master was not present, there was a glimmering fire on the stone, and the negligible canine was still resting before it. The air was warm and agreeable. He said I'm a fortunate man, scouring his hands. That is somewhat better. He saw the visitor book lying open, so he worked his name and tended to out of his cushion. Only two other passages were in this area, so he began perusing them as one generally accomplishes for guestbooks.

One was a Cardiffian Jeremy Sandler. The second was Bristol's, Gregory W. Sanctuary. He was saying unexpectedly, that's cool. Sandler. The Netherlands. It's like a hat. Now that very unusual name he'd seen on earth before? Was he a school kid? Actually, not so. Was this, maybe, a relative of his dad's, one of his sister's many young men? Yes, yes, none of these were. He glanced at this book again. He said softly, looking for his recollection, "Gregory Temple?" "Christopher, Sandler?" "Those beautiful children." And he replied by a voice that came from behind him, and in a twisted manner, he noticed his landlady walking into the hall, keeping it out in front of her, with a large silver tea tray.

"It sounded familiar," he said. "Did they? "I have seen those terms somewhere before, and I'm almost sure. This isn't queer? So, it was in the reports. In any sense, were they not renowned? Or something like that, I mean the popular cricketers and footballers?" "Ah, no, no, I don't believe they are popular. "Popular," she said as she placed the tea tray down on a table that was placed right in front of the sofa. Yet both of them were extremely beautiful, and I can tell you that. "It looked like it, I said, remembering the ages. It was large and young and beautiful, my friend, just as you said," Once again, Willy stared at the journal.

"The last reference is more than two years old."

"Oh, actually, yes."

"Lear me," she said, shaking her head from side to side, with a little sigh, "a little better." "I would not have heard of it any sooner. And Jeremy Sandler is almost a year before that, more than three years ago. How long does not, Mr. Wilkins, fly away from us all? "W-a-v-e-r." "Yes, it is, of course!" "W-a-v-e-r is Weaver." How ridiculous for me! She yelled, sitting on the couch. I've been excusing.

Mr. Weaver, it's me in one eye and outside the other." "Anything you know?" Willy replied," That's something exciting about all this?" Oh, you see both the words Sandler and Temple, not only I seem to tell you individually, so to say, but, in some particular way or another, they seem to be related to one another." Yes, you see both these terms, Sandler, and Temple. "So sweet," she said. "Oh, come then, little boy, and sit on the couch with me, and I'm going to give you a nice cup of tea and a biscuit before you go to sleep." "It shouldn't worry," Willy said. "I didn't mean that you should do something. I intend to do something. You're supposed to be the same thing." I am sure I'm going to.

"There's nothing more nervous than something like is that just outside the boundaries of one's mind. He despised giving up. Sandler...Christopher Sandler. Wasn't that a wandering title for the Eton college boy in the west, and then, "milk?" she said. "And sugar?" "Yeah. So unexpectedly," Eton schoolboy? Oh, my friend, that definitely couldn't be so because, when he came to me, my Mr. Sandler surely wasn't an Eton schoolboy. He's been a member of Oxford. Now come over and sit by me and warm up before this beautiful blaze. Go on. Move on. Keep on.

She patted on a couch next to her, and she just sat there with a beautiful smile on her face, patiently waiting for Willy's arrival. So, he crossed the room at a slow pace and quietly took a seat at the couch's far end. She positioned his cup of tea on the coffee table that was before him.

"It's where we are," she said.

"How beautiful and cozy is it, isn't it?" Willy is starting to drink his tea. She's been doing the same thing. For about forty-five seconds to a minute, none of them uttered a word to the other. Yet Willy was aware of how she stares at him. Willy's head is turning towards him halfway through, and he was able to feel her stare settling on his mouth, studying him from the bottom of his cup of tea."

She said, her brows arching.

"But he never left my beloved child. He is still here. He is still here. There's Mr. Temple, too." She slowly put her cup on the table and stared at his lucky lady, and then she grinned and put one of her white hands on her knee and patted it comfortably: "How old are you, my dear?" She inquired.

"Seventeen."

"Oh, that is a very ideal age!" She yelled.

At that point, Mr. Sandler was 17. Be that as it may, I don't accept the fact that he was a lot younger as compared to you, I am certain that he was, and he was not as white between his eyes.

"Mr. Weaver, did you know why you had the most delightful teeth?" They're not in the same class as they look," Willy said.

"We have only huge amounts of fillings as an afterthought," she included, not understanding, "yeah,

Mr. Sanctuary was somewhat more seasoned. In any case, on the unlikely chance that he didn't let me know, never in all my years, I wouldn't have known it. The skin had no blemishes."

"What?" Willy stated, his hair resembled that of a child."

There ended up being in a rearrangement of the schedule. Willy, in turn, decided to finish his tea and pour himself another cup. He took a small sip from it and placed it back on the coffee table. He sat tight for her to state whatever else, and it appeared as though she had slipped by in another of her hushes. The first time that I saw it from the street through the window, it fooled me. "Alas, no more!" he said, "The way it was done is most terribly smart." It doesn't look at least quite dead. I could have sworn that it was living. Who did that? Why did it?" I have." "You have done?

You saw my little Basil too," she said. "And of course?" Willy stared at it, and he suddenly realized that the creature was as still and behaving like the parrot all the time. He put his hand out and softly rubbed it on its paws. The back was durable and soft, and when he held his fur on his side with his hands, he could see the skin beneath white. "She turned towards the roof cat, who relaxed so peacefully in front of the fire. Were you going to have another teacup?" "Yes, thank you," said Willy. "The tea had mildly contained bitter almonds. I didn't care much about that." Yes." "It is good." Oh, yes. And now, I can generally descend here and look into when I begin to neglect what you were called. "Temple," Willy said. "Gregory Temple. I am as yet doing that pretty much consistently with Sandler and Mr. Temple." Excuse me for asking, yet in the last few years, there were no different guests here aside from them?" She kept her teacup in one hand high and marginally slanted her head to one side and gazed upward out the corners.

Priorities

Jack was a 65-year-old man who was rather proud of the life that he had built for his family. He had worked hard since his teenage years and done everything he could over the past five decades to give his family the life that he felt they deserved. He spent long hours working as a laborer, pulling in as many extra shifts as he could so that he could provide for his family. Thanks to his hard work, his wife was able to stay home and raise their three children in a beautiful home that he had purchased for them. He filled the home full of furniture, food, and various treasures based on whatever his family desired to have. When his family wanted to go on vacation, he would work overtime to afford the added expense and would always plan dreamy vacations that brought his family great joy. They would visit places like Disney Land, Martha's Vineyard, and even Arizona to see the desert. His family traveled to many different places enjoying all of the different views and creating many different memories.

Although he seemed to be around fairly frequently, Jack never felt as though he was able to truly relax and enjoy his time with his family. He had grown so used to working hard that he always had to be doing something: fixing something, building something, cleaning something, or moving something around. No matter what day it was or how much work he had already done, Jack would always do more work than what was reasonable because he simply felt uncomfortable just sitting around and enjoying the presence of his family. To Jack, nothing felt more satisfying than retiring after a hard day of working and feeling the comfort of his pillow rising to meet him.

One day, when he turned 66, Jack found that he was not feeling as good as he used to. For a while, he chalked it up to being older and dealing with regular pains of old age. After a few months, however, Jack could no longer deny that he was experiencing some fairly serious symptoms. His symptoms had grown so strong that he could no longer do the labor work that he once had, so he quit his job and retired to please his family. If it were up to him, Jack would have found a way to keep working despite his setbacks with his health. Still, he listened and retired, as he knew he probably should.

Shortly into his retirement, even simple things became challenging for Jack. He could no longer work like he used to, and eventually, even smaller tasks like climbing the stairs or going for a walk to the mailbox became more of a challenge for him. Finally, with his family's insistence, Jack went to visit a doctor to see why he might be experiencing such hardship with his health. It was from that appointment that Jack went on to learn that he was terminally ill with cancer and that he had waited too long to be checked so he was beyond the point of being able to be cured.

Jack and his family were shocked by this news as they realized that the once vital and virile man was quickly falling apart before their very eyes. Within weeks, Jack could no longer climb the stairs at all, and sometimes he even had trouble holding his coffee mug or pouring himself a glass of water. His wife, Susan, had to do everything for him. Being unable to do anything for himself made Jack angry and embarrassed, as he had always been a very proud and self-sufficient man. He spent the past five decades taking care of this woman; he did not feel as though he needed his wife to be taking care of him, now.

As time went on, Jack's anger turned into sadness. His family would all visit him in his home and bring their young children around, and everyone would play and get along like they always had. This time, though, Jack was forced to sit there and observe and partake in the conversation as he could no longer get up and find some work to do to keep himself busy. It was during these visits that Jack grew to understand just how much he had missed by being so deeply devoted to his work ethic and not spending enough time paying attention to his family. He realized that he had missed countless birthdays, holidays, anniversaries, and even just simple day-to-day memories because he was so absorbed in his need to work that he never truly sat down to enjoy his family until it was almost too late.

At first, Jack was angry with himself for not having spent more time with his family. He could not understand how foolish he had been by working so intensely and missing out on the majority of his children's and grandchildren's lives. Then, he became angry that he felt he had no choice but to work that hard to be able to give them the life that he wanted them all to enjoy. Eventually, Jack found himself thanking his own life for giving him enough time to see what he had missed and for giving him the opportunity to make up for it now before it was too late.

One day, when he was talking to his son, Jack decided to offer him some advice about his work ethic. Jack said, "Son when I was your age my priorities were all wrong.

I thought I had to work the hardest, be the best, and make the most money to make my family happy. Your mother told me she wanted me around more and wished I was there for the kids more, and I justified my actions by saying that I was there financially to support them. But that's not enough, son. In life, simply giving someone our money and hard work is not enough. If you truly want to be happy and live your best life, you take some time every single day to sit with those kids of yours and enjoy them. Never work so hard that you miss birthdays, anniversaries, or even just those special suppers each night. Be there for as many moments as you can, son, because believe me, one day they will have all slipped by. I realize now my priorities were wrong, and I taught you wrong. The true priority you need to have in life is to be able to provide for your family, but not just with finances. Prioritize the opportunity to provide them with your time, your attention, and your love. Believe me, son. It will make a world of difference."

Jack's son never forgot this story and went on to live by these words even long after Jack had passed. In fact, Jack's son went on to teach his own children about the value of these priorities, and they went on to teach their children! So, thanks to Jack and his hard work, his entire family was able to enjoy more quality time together for generations to come because he took the time to realize that prioritizing finances was not the only important thing in life. Time, attention, and love also mattered when it comes to providing for your family and truly taking care of them, and yourself.

The Sleep Fairy

There is a fairy out there whose magic powers help people sleep. Known simply as the Sleep Fairy, it flutters around, casting magic to put sleeps in everyone's eyes, and to help those who can't fall asleep finally do so. She uses her magic powers to help those in need, and with each person she helps, they thank the sleep fairy with a yawn, before falling asleep.

Every night, the sleep fairy finishes her nightly tasks with a pat on the back, satisfied with bringing the sleep to everyone in the land. She feels satisfied knowing everyone can sleep soundly, and not disturbed by the problems of the land.

However, the sleep fairy has a rival, the Insomniac. The Insomniac was the opposing force to the Sleep Fairy. Some say that the Insomniac was an evil twin of the Sleep Fairy, while others believe the Insomniac was crafted after a mad scientist who couldn't fall asleep wanted to wreak havoc on the world. If he couldn't sleep, no one could.

No matter the origin, however, both forces have clashed, trying to bring sleepiness or restlessness to the world.

This story was no exception, with both of these forces fighting with one another, although done in a way where the people who are trying to sleep don't notice. Instead, they either sleep soundly, or they wake up frustrated because the Insomniac didn't let them get the previous sleep they needed. For the most part, it's been an even match, that is until recently.

These days, it seems as though the Insomniac is winning. With today's technology, everything we do gives the Insomniac power and weakens the power of the Sleep Fairy. The Sleep Fairy tries and tries, and while she's had view victories, she's also suffered many losses too at the hands of the dastardly Insomniac.

Let me tell you an example. Our phones. This isn't a tale that is anti-technology, but it's how we use our technology that you should worry about. Many people are up all night, scrolling on social media, trying to give our brains stimulation through the next notification, email, or other updates. This puts our brains on hyperdrive, and it causes us to be restless when it's time to go to bed. The Insomniac then bets that you will continue being on your phones as you desperately try to look up how you can fall asleep, and the cycle repeats itself.

Plus, our worrying lifestyles make sleeping hard. We work long hours, worry about our job, and worry about not getting enough sleep, and this creates a tough cycle that the Insomniac uses to grow stronger. He put this cycle there and encourages people to be stressed about the lives they're living, of the problems they're suffering, because he knows that, with every person who wakes up improperly-rested, he too grows stronger.

The Sleep Fairy tries counteracting it every way she can. She encourages a hot bath, some herbal tea, and to do something that relaxes you rather than stimulates, but in this sleepless world, the Sleep Fairy's powers are not enough.

The Insomniac rules over quite a bit of this world, but the domain where he made his lair was the city of Tossturn. This was a thriving city, filled with everything to keep its people up at night. It was in a hot area, and the cost of electricity turned people away from a cool, crisp room that is needed for a nice night's sleep. The city of Tossturn was home to loud police sirens, people banging on their horns, and it was the city where everyone had to take a long commute to and from work. A city of screens and technology, it encouraged stimulation rather than sleep.

Everyone in this town put on extra makeup to hide the bags under their eyes, and it was not uncommon for people to drink so much energy drinks, they bled energy. This city's coffee shops were always jam-packed with people needing their fix, and car crashes and other accidents were common as well.

The Sleep Fairy hovered over this town. Every time she tried to get someone to fall asleep, her magic did not work. She waved her wand with a Z on top of it and tried to make a child fall asleep, but he was too busy on his game console to fall asleep.

One person sleeping at the job almost fell asleep, only for the boss to wake him up.

A woman was trying to fall asleep on a train, but then a yelling child woke her up. It was always something that kept everyone in Tossturn awake, and no matter what she did, her powers seemed weak. She knew that if she could just make everyone in this city fall asleep, the Insomniac would lose his power, but this was something that wasn't easy to do. She needed to think of a plan.

The Insomniac resided on top of the tallest building in Tossturn, the Empire Wake Building. There, he watched over this city, spreading his energy to everyone else in the town. Though no one could see him, the Sleep Fairy could. The Insomniac stood tall on the building, a mass of dark energy that could take any form he desired. Whatever kept you up at night, the Insomniac took the form of, and there was no stopping him.

However, the Sleep Fairy was determined to try. She knew that if the Insomniac grew more powerful, no one could sleep. However, the top of the Empire Wake Building was too high for her delicate little wings. She instead fluttered toward the entrance.

Everyone in these 24 hours town had jobs to do. They entered through the building, the revolving doors swinging. The Sleep Fairy went through the door, dodging the sleepy workers along the way. The inside of the building was quite spacious, with monitors everywhere. Monitors that emitted blue light that kept everyone up, destroying melatonin everywhere and preventing the restful sleep everyone deserved. She would stop them, no matter what.

The Sleep Fairy looked at the elevators. As soon as the doors opened, she flew in and flocked a bunch of people. She went inside, with everyone together like sardines as the door closed. This was just another day at the sleepless job, it seemed.

People in the elevator yawned, one of them almost sucking in the poor fairy. She went to the corner as the elevator went up, down, and in all directions, if it could. Eventually, there was an empty spot. Floor 42 was the floor she needed to go to.

She pressed on the button with all her might and up went the elevator. Up and up it went until it reached its proper destination. Then, it stopped, and she went out, breathing in the fresh, non-elevator air. This made her feel so nice, and she was ready to see what was on the next floor.

This floor was a computer room. Here, everyone not only did their business but in the back, there was a master computer system that controlled all the monitors around town. There was someone on the computer. They made a yawn, then passed out on the control panel for a little nap. Now or never. She had to do it now, or else she was never going to accomplish her goal.

The fairy pointed her wand at the monitor, which showed what every other monitor around the building displayed. Could her magic work?

It did not change. Whatever the Insomniac was using was powerful magic. Strong magic that held the monitor together. She had to act fast before the man woke up. She flipped her wand over and over, but nothing happened.

Then, she had an idea. She walked up to the napping man and whispered something in his ear. Although no one could hear or see the Sleep Fairy, she sometimes could communicate with humans when they were dreaming. Hopefully, this man was so tired that he was having a dream.

"Wake up!"

The man jarred awake as soon as she whispered. The manager scolded the poor worker as the Sleep Fairy fled to the elevator.

Once again, it was a ride in the world of elevators until she was able to go to the highest floor. Although the entrance to the rooftop was inaccessible for authorized personnel, there had to be a way to the top.

As soon as she exited, there was a long corridor. She looked up and saw a vent. Perfect. The Sleep Fairy squeezed her way through the vent, her wings fluttering as she popped right through it. Through tunnels she went, coughing up dust and avoiding some rats. This was the part where everything twisted and turned, winded back and forth until she went up and saw a way out.

Now, she was in a room that had a ladder in the corner. This ladder went down. She turned the knob, and there, she was at the roof.

The skyline of the city looked so beautiful. Many artificial lights decorated the place. If she didn't have some work to do, she would easily be able to enjoy the view. She shook her head and fluttered to the rooftop, and there, she saw the Insomniac.

In his default state, the Insomniac resembled a shadowy man with the color of dark roasted coffee beans. He looked to the skyline as well, and then looked to the fairy.

"So, Sleep Fairy. We meet at last. I was growing tired of waiting for you, unlike the citizens of this town."

The Sleep Fairy shook her head. "Why are you trying to do this? Don't you know that humans need sleep?

The Insomniac turned around. "Humans only want to sleep when they are dead. They are ambitious, drink the stuff to keep them awake, and they are always doing things to keep them up at night, such as looking at their computer screen. I just enhance the power of the things humans are already looking at. If they can live off of four hours of sleep each night, I see no harm."

"No," the Sleep Fairy retorted. "People need to sleep. They need to be able to get at least seven hours of sleep every night, and what you're doing is slowly hurting them. Sleep is the brain's way of refreshing itself, and you're out to destroy them!"

The Insomniac let out a chuckle. "Whatever you say. I do think humans are smart and can find a way to get all the sleep they need and still live. Perhaps there could be a world where no one needs sleep. Imagine a machine that could refresh you in seconds."

The fairy clenched her fist. "People need some time to unwind and rest, and they need time to dream. Dreams help humans grow and realize their full potential. If they aren't dreaming, then they aren't going to accomplish their goals in life."

"Say what you will," the Insomniac said. "The only way to resolve this is to fight it out."

The Insomniac lunged towards the fairy, and the Sleep Fairy fluttered out of the way. She countered by waving her wand and shooting out the dust of sleepiness at the Insomniac. However, the Insomniac just brushed it off like crusts in his eyes.

"Your pixie dust magic is too weak," he said. "Now, let me show you my power."

The Insomniac started to change shape. His body stretched and became without any form. Like a balloon with too much air, he began towering over the roof, like a malformed King Kong ready to strike. He swung his fist and smacked the Sleep Fairy. She flew off the roof, and almost fell off the building, but managed to regain her consciousness. She flew upwards, but just as she did, the Insomniac grabbed her torso. She tried breaking out, but her grip was too strong. She felt like she could pop like a cherry tomato if she stayed like this for too long.

"You tried to defeat me," the Insomniac said. His face all twisted, barely resembling anyone's visage at all, a long tongue came from his maw.

"I don't know if I want to crush you like a bug or eat you like one. You know, swallowing you alive sounds pretty tasty."

He licked his lips, black goo coming from his tongue, and then his tongue grew closer and closer to the Sleep Fairy.

The Sleep Fairy's sighed. Well, it was fun. She had a fun time letting all the humans sleep. All those good memories she had. Children who were all wound up fell asleep as soon as she read them stories. Adults who were worried about tomorrow fell asleep without worry. It was a good time, but she assumed that everything had to come to a close. She wondered how humanity could carry on without sleep, but like the Insomniac said, maybe, just maybe, everyone could find their way.

The sound of rain filled the city. Was it raining? And yet, she did not feel a single drop on her.

All of a sudden, the grip on her loosened, and she squeezed out. The Insomniac winced a bit, and she looked around.

All the monitors in the city changed. Once bright, blue light, they were now light that was a warm color that made everyone in the town yawn looking at it. From the speakers, a soothing noise of rain played. She saw everyone leaving the buildings, rushing to get back to their homes. In no time, there were lights in the apartment buildings, and then the lights turned off. The city's lights began dimming all over.

"What did you do?" he shouted; his form unable to contain itself. He grew, expanded, then shrunk, then repeated the process.

"The sleeping worker heard me after all," she murmured.

The Insomniac's body shrunk and shrunk until it was the size of a man once again. However, the body still tried expanding. The Sleep Fairy went to the Insomniac, then pointed her wand.

"Go to sleep," she said. "Just like everyone else."

The Insomniac looked at her, his empty eyes filled with a noticeable contempt.

"You may have defeated me for now, but sleeplessness will always happen. I will be back, and when I do, I'll make sure no one gets any sleep."

"You may never go away, but when you do wake up, I'll be ready."

The Sleep Fairy pointed the wand at the Insomniac, and then declared, "Good night."

The Insomniac's empty eyes closed, and his form shrank again. What was left was a baby-shaped blob of dark matter, sleeping soundly. It almost looked cute, in away. The Sleep Fairy then conjured up a bed and laid the Insomniac to rest. With a mighty wave, the bed flew off the building and into the Land of Dreams, where she hoped the Insomniac would rest for a long, long time.

As the Sleep Fairy looked the quiet city, she yawned herself. "Guess it's time for me to go to bed," she said.

She disappeared into the land of dreams. There, she went to one of the many clouds and pulled the cloud over her like a blanket. As she thought about the day, she realized that indeed, her work would never be done. There would always be someone who could not sleep, and there would always be someone who needed the help of the Sleep Fairy.

Be it a child who needed to go to school tomorrow, a teen who spent too much time out late, a college student who procrastinated, an adult worrying about the future, or an older adult thinking about the past, someone would always be up.

And to the sleep fairy, that was okay. She would make sure the Insomniac would never return again. With that, she closed her eyes, and let her own body go to sleep. Her muscles relaxed, her head sunk into the cool, crisp pillow, and she cleared her mind. Now, she floated down the river in a never-ending sea of sleepiness and dreams.

Conclusion

Thank you for making time for Bedtime Stories for Adults and let's hope it was helpful and able to provide you with all of the tools you need to achieve your goals whatever they may be.

Your journey of centeredness, wholeness, and balance will move forward as you continue to support yourself through these meditation practices.

You can use them anytime you need to in order to find the restfulness you are looking for, to help you unravel and unwind your thoughts and begin to rejoice in the feeling of total relaxation.

The best part of using these tools and resources is that you are able to change your present state of anxiety, tension, worry, or stress in a matter of minutes, just by shutting off the outside world for several minutes, going within, and exploring your deeper mind and consciousness, acquiring the self-healing tools you need to feel refreshed every day and every night.

You can begin to achieve the calmness of mind, body, and spirit that lifts you higher and higher into your truest state of being, allowing you to fully rest and replenish your energy, helping you to feel prepared for anything life hands you.

Continue to work with these guided meditations as a way to find comfort, peace of mind, and healing power from within.

Bedtime Stories for Adults will give you all of the serenity and soothing comfort you need to fall asleep, heal your mind and spirit, and find your wholeness every day.

CPSIA information can be obtained
at www.ICGtesting.com
Printed in the USA
BVHW060945070122
625664BV00012B/246